Volume 2

by Dr. Mac & Friends

Songs, Activities, and A Lot of Fun for Kids Ages 4–9

Lyrics and music by Dr. Mac, a.k.a. Don R. MacMannis, Ph.D.
Activities written by Debbie M. O'Neal

free spirit
PUBLiSHiNG®

Helping kids
help themselves™
since 1983

Music and Lyrics Copyright © 2007, 2003 by Don R. MacMannis, Ph.D.
Text Copyright © 2007 by Free Spirit Publishing Inc.

All rights reserved under International and Pan American Copyright Conventions. The purchase of this book entitles the buyer to reproduce song lyrics and activity sheets for home or classroom use only—not for commercial use or resale, and not for an entire school or school district/system. Copying of the CD is strictly prohibited, as is the storage of any of the material in a retrieval system or transmittal of the material in any form or by any means electronic, mechanical, recording, or otherwise, without express written permission of the publisher.

Free Spirit, Free Spirit Publishing, and associated logos are trademarks and/or registered trademarks of Free Spirit Publishing Inc. A complete listing of our logos and trademarks is available at www.freespirit.com.

ISBN-13: 978-1-57542-245-9
ISBN-10: 1-57542-245-X

Editor, John Kober ★ Designers, Marieka Heinlen and Tasha Kenyon ★ Illustrator, Brie Spangler

10 9 8 7 6 5 4 3 2 1
Printed in Hong Kong

Free Spirit Publishing Inc.
217 Fifth Avenue North, Suite 200
Minneapolis, MN 55401-1299
(612) 338-2068
help4kids@freespirit.com
www.freespirit.com

Free Spirit Publishing is a member of the Green Press Initiative, and we're committed to printing our books on recycled paper containing a minimum of 30% post-consumer waste (PCW). For every ton of books printed on 30% PCW recycled paper, we save 5.1 trees, 2,100 gallons of water, 114 gallons of oil, 18 pounds of air pollution, 1,230 kilo-watt hours of energy, and .9 cubic yards of landfill space. At Free Spirit it's our goal to nurture not only young people, but nature too!

Acknowledgments

The second volume of *Ready to Rock Kids* has been enhanced by some exciting new elements. Brian Mann, the best "partner" a guy could ever have, has added his creativity to the production, arrangements, vocal direction, and song writing. A new member of our musical team, Craig Dobbin, also has contributed his amazing talents to the arrangements.

I have cherished my relationship with the kids in this project. Most people aren't aware of the thousands of hours that go into music like this, but the kids in our chorus are! Months of Sunday afternoon rehearsals and recording sessions taught us all how to bring out the best in each other. Truly the backbone of this effort, they were amazing! Many thanks also to their families for their support and encouragement.

Also indispensable to our latest and greatest sound is the participation of some new adult singers, with Lois Mahalia, Eje Lynn-Jacobs, Red Steagall, Michelle Lawyer, and Kirstin Candy all playing major roles. As with the other fine players, guitarist Mike Miller added his magic to the final sound.

Thanks, as always, to my wife, Debra, for her guidance and support, and to my mom and sisters for their endless enthusiasm. I am indebted to Daniel Goleman, Ph.D., Maurice Elias, Ph.D., Ron Taffel, Ph.D., Becky Beiley, and all of my numerous friends and advisors. Finally, a big thanks to my new friends at Free Spirit Publishing—especially Judy, John, Phil, Marieka, Tasha, Debbie, and Brie—all of whom gave their hearts and souls, synergistically, to help create this, my second dream come true.

—Dr. Mac

Produced by Dr. Mac with Brian Mann and Craig Dobbin
Arrangements by Brian Mann and Craig Dobbin
Vocal arrangements by Dr. Mac and Brian Mann

Lyrics and music by Dr Mac: tracks 1, 2, 6, 8, 9, 10, 11, 12
Lyrics and music by Dr. Mac and Brian Mann: tracks 3, 4, 5, 7

Children's Chorus Solo Tracks

Emma Steinkellner 1, 2, 4, 5, 7
Olivia Fanaro 1, 2, 4, 7, 9
Allison Lewis 9, 10
Sam Kulchin
Briggs Boss 1, 2, 4
Anya Ruskin 1, 2, 4
Patricia Westley 1, 2
Addison Mills 2

Adult Lead and Solo Vocal Tracks

Dr. Mac 1, 4, 5, 6, 7, 8, 10, 11, 12
Lois Mahalia 3, 11
Eje Lynn-Jacobs 11
Red Steagall 6
Kirstin Candy 11
Michelle Lawyer 4, 11
Kathryn Ish 4

Child Narrations and Rap Tracks

Nya Burke 2, 4, 7, 11
Alexandra Varner 1, 2, 4, 11
Aaron Linker 2, 4, 11
Kelly Adams 2, 4, 11
Miguel Leon 2

Adult Background Vocal Tracks

Dr. Mac 3, 4, 6, 7, 8, 10, 11, 12
Lois Mahalia 3, 7, 11, 12
Eje Lynn-Jacobs 3, 7, 11, 12
Kirstin Candy 7, 11, 12
Michelle Lawyer 3, 4, 11
Sean MacMannis 3, 11
Debra Manchester 4, 11
Kirk Taylor 7, 11
Brian Mann 8
Leslie Spencer 4, 11
Betty Mann 4

Musicians

Brian Mann keyboards, programming, all instruments, accordion
Craig Dobbin keyboards, programming, all instruments
David West banjo and mandolin track 6
Mike Miller electric and acoustic guitars
Dan Zimmerman electric guitar track 8
Craig Thomas saxophone track 1
Tom Ball harmonica track 9
DJ Radius turntable track 2

Engineered by Eric Palmquist and Tom Flowers
Recorded at Orange Whip Studios, Mann Made Studios, and Craig Dobbin Studios
Mixed by Brian Mann, Craig Dobbin, and Dr. Mac
Mastered by Doug Sax

Contents

Introduction · · · · · · · · · · · · · · · · · 4

Song Lyrics and Activity Pages

Bye, Bye Bully · · · · · · · · · · · · · · 6
Sailing on the Seven Cs · · · · · · 8
The Gift of Giving · · · · · · · · · · 10
Let 'Em Out · · · · · · · · · · · · · · 12
The Carousel Song · · · · · · · · · 14
The Golden Rule · · · · · · · · · · · 16
Same and Different Too · · · · · 18
What You Can Do · · · · · · · · · · 20
Sharing Friends · · · · · · · · · · · 22
I Don't Understand · · · · · · · · · 24
Cleanup Time · · · · · · · · · · · · · 26
Soldier of Peace · · · · · · · · · · · 28

Fun Things to Do Together

Bye, Bye Bully · · · · · · · · · · · · 30
Sailing on the Seven Cs · · · · · 31
The Gift of Giving · · · · · · · · · · 33
Let 'Em Out · · · · · · · · · · · · · · 34
The Carousel Song · · · · · · · · · 36
The Golden Rule · · · · · · · · · · · 37
Same and Different Too · · · · · 39
What You Can Do · · · · · · · · · · 40
Sharing Friends · · · · · · · · · · · 41
I Don't Understand · · · · · · · · · 43
Cleanup Time · · · · · · · · · · · · · 44
Soldier of Peace · · · · · · · · · · · 45

Introduction

The inspiration for *Ready to Rock Kids* came from asking young children about the music they like to listen to. Kids are quite sophisticated these days and are attracted to the quality and rhythm of popular young adult music, which is often lyrically inappropriate for them.

The full-production songs of *Ready to Rock Kids* are both highly entertaining and age appropriate—adult quality music, but with words and themes to which kids can really relate. The different adult and child soloists, children's chorus, and wide range of instruments and styles of music easily hold children's attention.

We live in an age where high stress, the media, and pop culture often have a negative influence on children, but now we also have the know-how to help them thrive through it all. As a child psychologist, I know that giving kids tools to help them feel good about themselves and get along with others helps them to be happy, and happy kids learn better!

Teachers are often overwhelmed with the problems that keep children from learning in the academic subjects. They realize that an important way to help the children overcome the problems is to do a better job teaching character education. Parents, too, want to do a better job at teaching these same values and character traits. Now there is an engaging way to do just that. The songs and activities in this book are fun, positive learning tools that support children's social and emotional development.

Most of us remember the words to songs we heard as young children. Don't you still sing the ABC song in your head when you're trying to remember alphabetical order? There may be no more powerful method of learning than through music, and no more important lessons for children than those that focus on social and emotional skills.

—Dr. Mac

"Be aware of wonder. Live a balanced life — learn some and think some and draw and paint and sing and dance and play and work every day some."

— Robert Fulghum

How to use this book and CD

The songs and activities in this book address the following themes:

★ inclusion and cooperation ★ celebrating diversity ★ giving and receiving ★ dealing with bullies
★ responsibility ★ teamwork ★ peacemaking ★ happiness ★ practice

You will find many ways to use both this book and CD in the classroom, at home, or on the go. One easy thing to do in the classroom is to play the CD at quiet or less-structured times throughout the day, such as when students arrive or during art classes. At home, listen to the CD while playing or while driving in your car—a fun way for kids and parents to learn the songs and talk together about what is important in living together as a family.

Research shows that "layering" concepts and related activities and experiences increases the likelihood that those concepts will become an integral part of who we are. Any time we integrate activities and concepts across the curriculum, there is a better chance of retaining, transferring, and understanding the information. Integrate the songs into your music curriculum, perhaps choosing a song of the week to learn the words and music. As you listen to the songs and review the related activities in this book, you will see that they can easily be integrated into many areas of your curriculum. For example, use the book suggestions with each song in language arts, use the song "Cleanup Time" at the end of the day, and use all of the songs when teaching character traits in social studies.

How this book is organized

❶ In the first section, for each of the 12 songs, a lyrics page and a child's activity page reinforces a key concept of the song. These pages may be reproduced to help kids learn the song and understand its message. For easy use by children, this 24-page section has been placed at the front of the book, apart from the adult-directed activities at the back of the book.

❷ The second section, beginning on page 30, is a collection of activities for each individual song. These hands-on learning experiences, for use at school or home, reinforce the key concepts of the songs, which you will see listed on the activity pages. The activities include the following features:

- ▷ Activities are provided across the span of ages 4 to 9. Some will be more appropriate for younger, and some for older, children. You can adapt the activities by age level as needed.

- ▷ With each song is a suggested book to read and talk about, which helps in layering (see above) the key concept with kids. The books are easily found in libraries or at many bookstores. Use the book suggestion, or others you know that address the song's concept, to stimulate more thought and discussion with your child or children.

- ▷ The activities include arts and crafts, movement, drama, and games. It will be easy to make adjustments in the activities for age level, as well as time and space constraints. Use these ideas as a springboard for you and the kids to think of new and creative ways to learn together.

- ▷ Some activities will require you to gather basic supplies. The materials suggested in most cases are readily available around school or home. In some cases you may know of a way to adapt the activity for use with other materials. A good practice is to always try the activity yourself before using it with children.

Bye, Bye Bully

Na na na na na, Na na na na na.
Once I knew a boy named Beau
Who lived on a farm. Where? I don't know,
But a bully came and called him a name,
And tried to get his goat.

Once I knew a boy named Blake
Who rowed a boat on a little lake
'Til a bully came and called him a name,
And tried to rock his boat.

Hey you, cut it out;
Your names are not about me.
I'll walk away with my head up high,
And say, by the way, nice try. (Nice try.)

And I once knew a girl named, Kim
Who was climbing up on a jungle gym,
When a bully came and called her a name,
And tried to tease her down.

Hey you, please, cut it out;
Your teasin's not about me.
I'll walk away with my head up high,
And say, by the way, nice try. Nice try.

Don't let 'em get your goat or rock your boat
Or get the best of you.
They're just looking for love in the weirdest way
With what they say or do,
Be do be do be do be do.

Hey you, cut it out,
And if you can't, you'll be without me,
'Cause I'll walk away with my head up high,
And say, by the way, good-bye. Nice try.

Bye, bye bully. (repeated)
Names will never hurt me, no matter what you say.
I'll tell the teacher, 'cause it's not okay.
I'll just ignore you, no matter what you say.
A bully's just unhappy, and havin' a bad day. (Poor bully.)

Circle the words from the list that you find hidden in the puzzle. How many can you find?

Word list:
- FRIEND
- BULLY
- CARING
- RESPECT
- HAPPY
- LOVE
- GOODBYE
- TOGETHER

```
X F E D Y L T M K T
M Y R L A R O D Q O
T C L I E P M V R G
D U E P E A U C E E
B Y L Y J N V A S T
Q E U L S S D R P H
A D A Y J T Z I E E
G O O D B Y E N C R
H A P P Y U W G T X
Z I F R D T M N E E
```

Sailing on the Seven Cs

(Chorus)
When we're sailing on the good ship, friendship,
We're sailing off on a breeze.
When we're sailing on the good ship, friendship,
We're sailing on the seven Cs.

C stands for *caring* and *consideration*.
C stands for *commitment* and *communication*.
Just add *concern, curiosity,* and *cooperation,*
And you've got the creation of the seven Cs.

Caring means to keep your friends in your heart,
Be thinking about them, together or apart.
Consideration means to learn about their needs,
Consider their feelings and do good deeds.

Commitment means that you never have a doubt.
When the going gets tough, you work things out.
Communication means that you say what you feel,
And when you do it nicely, then it's no big deal.

(Chorus)

Concern just means the same as caring,
Not much blame and lots of sharing.
Curiosity means finding out,
What your friend is all about.
And *cooperation* never ends,
Sailing together on the good ship of friends.

(Chorus)

Caring—sailing on the seven Cs, *Consideration*—sailing on the seven Cs, *Commitment*—sailing on the seven Cs, *Communication*—sailing on the seven Cs, *Concern*—sailing on the seven Cs, *Curiosity*—sailing on the seven Cs, *Cooperation*—sailing on the seven Cs.

Add the missing letters to spell the seven Cs.
You will need to add five of each of these letters: **I, N, O, R, T.**
Color the border to make a mini-poster!

**caring, consideration, commitment, communication,
concern, curiosity, cooperation.**

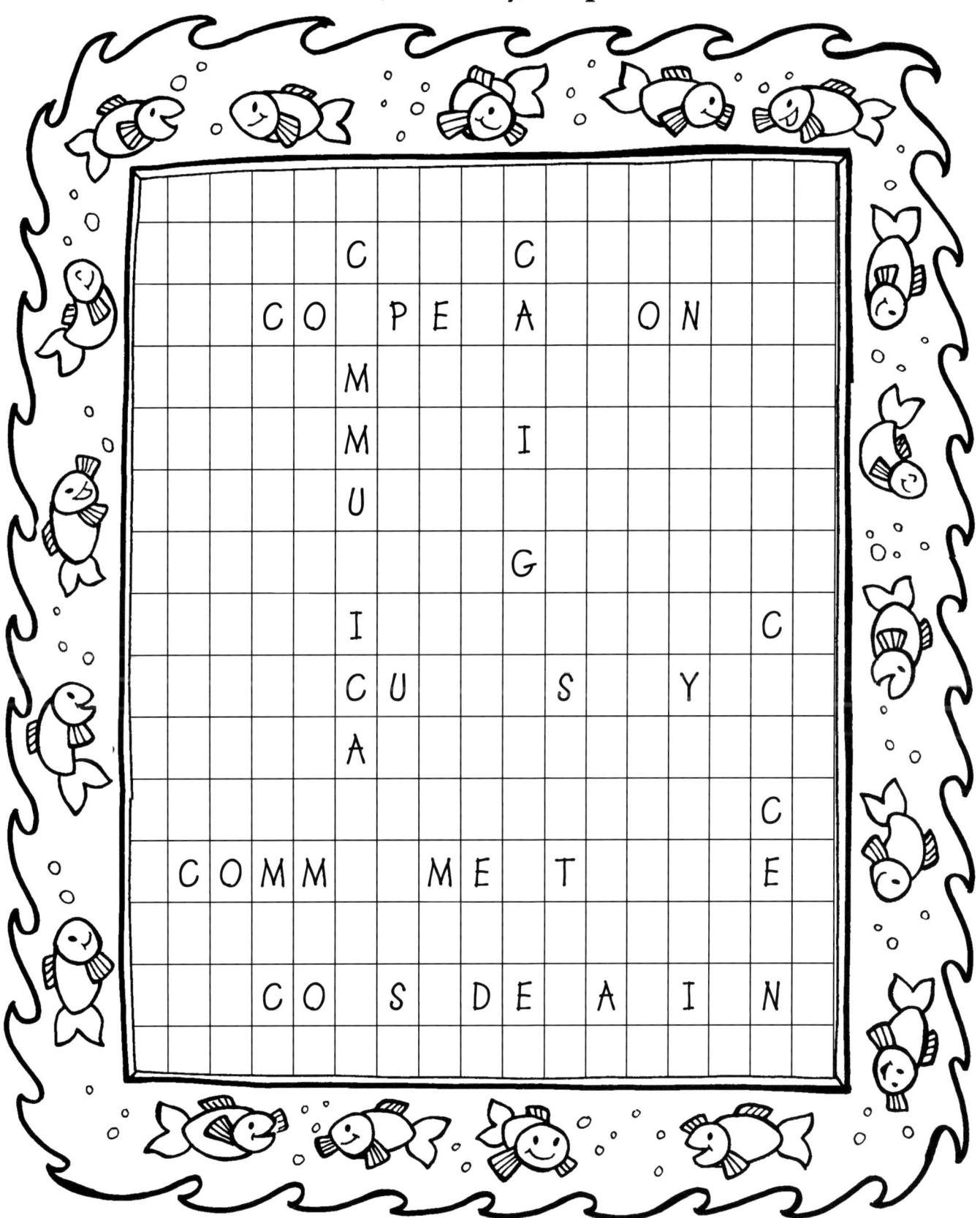

The Gift of Giving

Just like a snowball that grows when it rolls,
And just like the mountains with winter snows,
And just like a baby elephant's nose,
Love grows.

Just like a forest will reach for the sky,
And just like the oceans can never run dry,
And just like the children asking why,
Love grows.

And there's a gift of giving, and so it goes,
That with the gift of giving,
Love grows and grows and grows.

Silly as one plus one makes three,
But that's how it happens and
It's meant to be,
When I give to you, I give to me. Love grows.

Yeah, it's the gift of giving, and so it goes,
That with the gift of giving,
Love grows and grows and grows.

It's the silliest thing that you'd ever suppose,
'Cause it grows when it's given away.
Just ask any candle how sharing its light
Can turn the night into day.

It's the gift of giving, and so it goes,
That with the gift of giving,
Love grows and grows and grows.

And it's a way of living, and heaven knows;
A little gift of giving, and love grows
And grows and grows.

And it's the gift of giving, and so it goes,
With the gift of giving, love grows and
Grows and grows and grows and grows.

Color the picture.

Let 'Em Out

Just like a sneeze has got a reason to achoo,
Feelings want a way to come out.
Just find the words to say what'll make 'em go away;
Let 'em out, let 'em out, let 'em out.

Sometimes I'm lonely; sometimes I'm sad;
Sometimes my feelings get hurt.
The hardest time for me is when I'm acting bad,
And then I lose my dessert.

(Chorus)
Just like a sneeze has got a reason to achoo,
Feelings want a way to come out.
Just find the words to say what'll make 'em go away;
Let 'em out, let 'em out, let 'em out, let 'em out.

My little sister Susan's the best,
But she waits 'til I'm walkin' to school.
Then she plays in my room and leaves it a mess,
Then I'll be losin' my cool.

(Chorus)

Just like giggles make you wiggle about, or excitement makes you shiver and shout,
Like a baby about to be born, or a movie theater poppin' some corn,
Like a puppy wants to go for a walk,
You got some good news and you gotta talk,
Like a seed reachin' up for the sky, a baby bird that's itchin' to fly,
Like rain comin' down from the clouds, or a burp that's gotta burp its way out,
Let 'em out, let 'em out, let 'em out, let 'em out.

(Chorus – 2 times)

Fill in the blanks with words that tell how you are feeling. Then draw a face in the circle to show that feeling.

Today I am feeling _____

_____

Something that makes me happy is _____

_____

Something that makes me sad is _____

_____

When I am lonely, I like to _____

_____

When I am happy, I like to _____

_____

I get angry when _____

_____

The Carousel Song

It's eight o'clock on a soccer day,
And I'm barely awake.
I've got a shot that I can make,
But I'm afraid I'll make a mistake.

It's ten o'clock and I forgot the way
To ride my bike.
Then I remembered my grandpa say
That's what life is like.

(Chorus)
Life is like a bowl of cherries
When things are going well.
And life is like a breeze that carries you.
And life is like a carousel,
Yeah, kind of like a carousel.

Another time, another day,
I fell down on a hike.
But I remembered my grandpa say
That's what life is like!

(Chorus)

And who could ever know what's comin' around
With all the ups and downs life sends.
Just jump on a painted pony,
And if you fall, just jump up again.

Life is like a bowl of cherries
When things are going well.
And life is like a breeze that carries you.
And life is like a carousel,
At least as far as I can tell.
And life is like a carousel,
Yeah, kind of like a carousel.

Round and round, and round and round,
And round and round, and round and round . . .

Life is like a carousel,
What comes 'round you can never tell,
Round and round like a carousel,
And I wish you well, I wish you well.

Follow the dots from 1 to 50 to finish the picture. Then color the picture.

The Golden Rule

Ba ohm boppa doo, ba ohm boppa doo,
Ba ohm boppa doo badoo (2 times).

If you want to be my friend,
Well, there's one thing that's got to end.
Your teasing me's just not okay,
So let's go find another way.

Well, yes, I want to be your friend.
And a better way's around the bend.
Well, I was bein' bad and cool, and what a fool.
And I forgot the Golden Rule. What's that?

Just do to others what you would like them to do
To you, that's what you do.
It's like my momma said with her Southern drawl,
"Y'all say somethin' nice or nothin' at all."

You just do to others what you
Would like them to do to you;
Yeah, that's what we'll do.
Just like my momma said, clear as I can recall,
She said, "Say somethin' nice or nothin' at all."

It's so good you're gonna be my friend.
We'll be together 'til the very end.
Knowin' life the way we do,
Me and you'll be goin' by that Golden Rule.

The Golden Rule, ooo, ooo, ooo (4 times).

Say something NICE, or NOTHING at all.

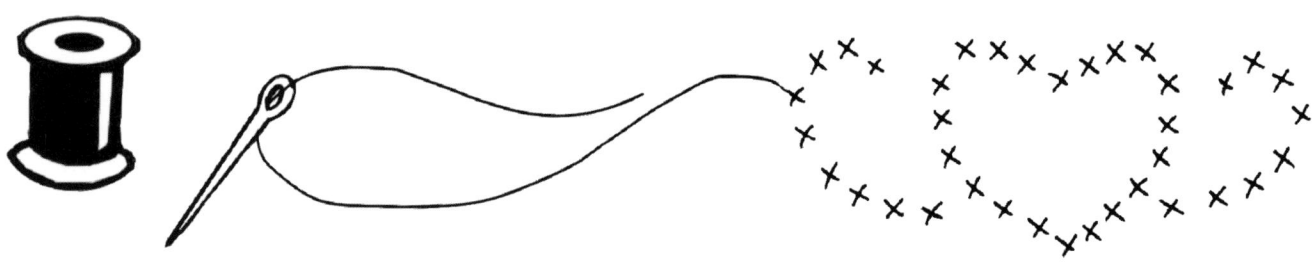

Color the words and frame. Hang it in your room or give it to a friend.

Same and Different Too

Same and different too, same and different too.
I like it when it's cloudy;
Well, I like it when it's clear.
I like it when it's raining;
I like when rainbows appear.

We like the sounds of the city;
They like the country the best.
We like those eastern oceans;
They like the ones in the west.

Though we're so much the same,
We're different too,
Different names and points of view,
But lots of things we all like to do.
Same and different too, same and different too.

Different singers in the same band,
Different fingers on the same hand,
Different pieces of the same pie,
Different but the same, you and I.

Though we're so much the same, we're different too,
Just the same and different too.
Same and different too, same and different too.

Different shells from the same shore,
Different socks from the same drawer,
Different stars from the same sky,
Different but the same, you and I.

Different smiles from the same face,
Different sounds from the same bass,
Different ones from the same two, we're just the same.
Same and different, same and different,
Same and different too.
Same and different too.
Same and different too.
Same and different too.

Think about yourself and a friend. In the part of the circles that overlap, list all the things that are the same about you and your friend. In the two parts of the circles that don't overlap, list some things or qualities that describe one of you but not the other.

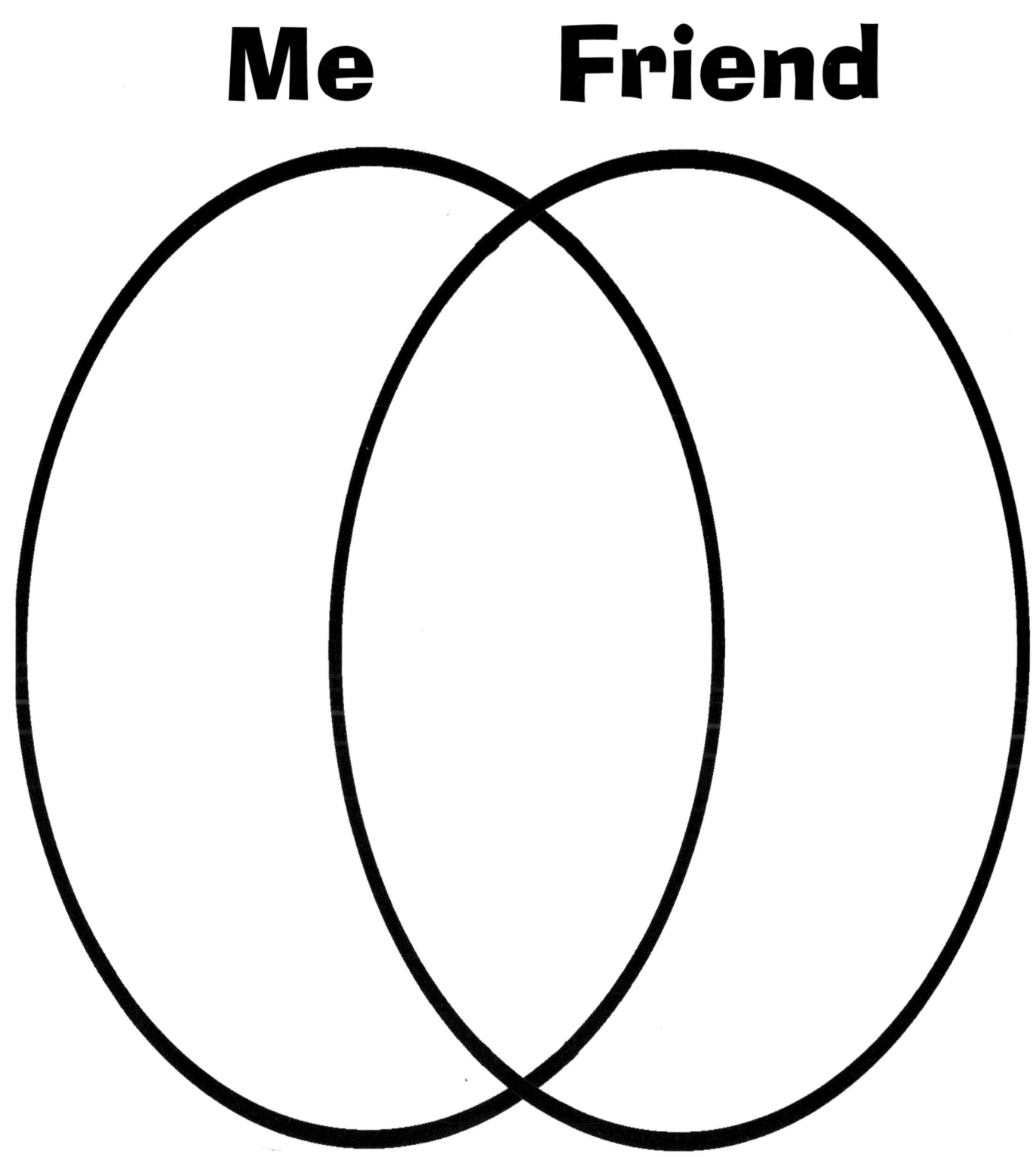

What You Can Do

I know you want to be careful.
We'll take a step at a time,
And you can still be careful
And make this climb.

Some things can be scary,
Especially the first time.
But follow me, and you will see
That it's fine.

And if you never try,
You'll never know.
You'll never understand new things
And how they go.

But if you take a chance
With something new,
Just take a turn and you can learn
What you can do.

And when you try
Well, then you'll know.
You'll understand new things,
And how they go.
And if you take a chance
With something new,
Just take a turn and you can learn
What you can do.

You just take a turn, and you can learn
What you can do.

Why don't you try it, and you'll learn,
Why don't you try it, and you'll learn,
Why don't you try it, and you'll learn,
What you can do.

Why don't you try it, and you'll learn
What you can do.

All of these things grow. Finish the pictures and then color them.

Sharing Friends

If you want to play with Marie,
Play with her and not with me,
It's not what I want, but it's okay,
And I'll come back another day.

Just a moment, wait a second,
I can ask Marie and check and
See if she would really care
If you would join, and we would share.

So I just checked and she said "yes,"
So let's all play, come be our guest,
'Cause sharing friends is the way to go.
I'm glad we all said "yes" instead of "no."
I'm glad we all said "yes" instead of "no."

Yes, yeah, yeah. Yes, yeah, yeah (2 times).
I'm glad we all said "yes" instead of "no."

Color the picture of friends playing together.

I Don't Understand

I don't understand.

Teacher, won't you please explain
How floating clouds can make the falling rain
Come down upon the ground?
Please explain.

And teacher, help me feed my brain.
It isn't dumb, but it's become so plain
To see it's driving me insane.
With wondering why, I'm wondering why, so say, 'cause . . .

(Chorus)
I don't understand why birds can fly.
If anything can, then why can't I?
Give me an answer, give it a try.
Won't you tell me, 'cause I don't understand?

I don't understand.

So teacher, won't you please explain?
If there's a plan and if you can
Explain it to me, then I won't be complaining
And wondering why; I keep wondering why,
So say, 'cause . . .

(Chorus two times)

I don't know why birds can fly,
But if they can, then why can't I?
Give an answer, give it a try,
Won't you tell me?

(Chorus)

Teacher, won't you tell me? No, I don't understand. (3 times)

Draw pictures of the people who answer your questions and teach you. Then color the frame.

Cleanup Time

If everybody starts to run away
Each time they hear me say, "It's cleanup time,"
Then when that happens there's a price to pay,
'Cause for the ones that stay it's such a crime.

There's too much work for one, and too much work for two,
Too much work for three or even four.
But we can get it done; yeah, we can get through.
And we can make it fun and not a chore.

Cleanup time can be fun when there's help from everyone. (2 times)

Please pick up those puzzle pieces under the chair.
I'll have some fun finding the ones that fell over there.
Oh, I'll put those instruments all back in the box.
I'll get the toys; I'll get the games, and I'll get those blocks.

Putting things back where they belong, putting things back with the cleanup song.
When things go back and put away, then they're there for another day.
Pieces of paper on the floor, some for the trash, some for the drawer.
Some can clean the art supplies. Hey what about clean the other guy's?

You get the socks and shoe and I'll get the clothes,
And put 'em in the closet where everybody knows they go.
Who lost a jacket? And here's somebody's comb.
Let's put 'em in our backpacks, yeah, and take 'em, home.

Bottles and cans, some papers too, not in the trash, not what to do!
Put them in the bin, put them in the bin, for the recyclin', the recyclin'.
Everybody wins when we all pitch in; yeah, finish the job before we begin.
No more mess, no more rhyme, seems like the end of cleanup time.
Cleanup time, cleanup time, cleanup time, cleanup time.
Hey, cleanup time. Everybody pitch in, it's a good thing!
Cleanup time can be fun when there's help from everyone.

SILVER LAKE PARK PUZZLE

What is wrong with this picture? Circle the things that show how people are not taking care of the world. What would you do differently?

Soldier of Peace

Now we've come to the final part
When you open up and fill your heart
With light, and then you'll start
To be a soldier, a soldier of peace.

Yes, now we've come to the final part
When you close your eyes and find your star.
Become the light you are
As a soldier, a soldier of peace.

If we can find understanding
Instead of finding faults,
Then we can keep building bridges
Instead of building walls.

(Chorus)
Come join up, extend a hand
Around the world, across the land.
Put your heart first in command, and
Be a soldier, a soldier of peace.

If we can find understanding
Instead of finding faults,
Then we can keep building bridges
Instead of building walls.

(Chorus)

A soldier of peace. (3 times)

Every day our hearts can play;
We'll find a way to love one another,
Every sister and brother,
Every father and mother,
Every daughter and son,
Everyone, everyone.

One, we're one, one.
Love is the way.
Love one another,
Every sister and brother.
We're one.

Be a peacemaker with your friends! Color the words and draw yourself and your friends into the picture.

Fun Things to Do Together

Bye, Bye Bully

Focus: Dealing with bullies

Social and Emotional Concepts:

⇨ Teasing others can hurt their feelings.

⇨ People are different, but no one is better than anyone else.

⇨ Teasing others is not the right thing to do.

> **A Book to Read and Talk About**
> It is almost April Fools Day, and Arthur is ready for the big show. But what happens when there is a bully in the audience? Find out in *Arthur's April Fool* by Marc Brown.

Heart Breaker

In advance of this activity, cut a large heart from red construction paper or tissue paper.

Even if a person's intention by teasing is to have fun, it can often hurt someone's feelings.

Ask each child to sign the heart. Then have the kids, one at a time, pretend to tease and say something, in the abstract, that might hurt a person's feelings. With each response, crumple a little bit of the heart. When all the children have responded, the heart should be in a crumpled ball.

Next, have each child say something that would make a friend feel good. With each positive comment, open a little more of the paper heart. When finished, the heart will be back to normal—almost. Discuss why there are still wrinkles in the heart, and then have the children name ways that things can get ironed out in relationships, and thus healing our hearts.

Point out how we all have the ability to say and do both positive and negative things. Choose to do the positive!

Bully Practice

After playing the song "Bye, Bye Bully" a number of times, divide the children into four groups and assign each group to sing one of the last four lines:

Group 1: "Names will never hurt me, no matter what you say."
Group 2: "I'll tell the teacher, 'cause it's not okay."
Group 3: "I'll just ignore you, no matter what you say."
Group 4: "A bully's just unhappy, and havin' a bad day."
Everyone: "Poor bully."

First have each group rehearse its line a few times. Now as you play the whole song, have everyone sing the choruses and then let each group sing its part alone at the appropriate time. Everyone gets to say "Poor bully."

Bully Free

You will need The Bully Free™ Card Game *available from Free Spirit Publishing.*

Use the card game, which is played like Crazy Eights, to help kids learn anti-bullying concepts in a fun way. By exploring potential bullying situations, kids can offer reasonable suggestions for ways to stay bully free.

Name Mobiles

You will need a plastic clothes hanger for each child, clear adhesive paper, markers, drawing paper, scissors, hole punch, nylon fishing thread or paper clips.

To reinforce that a child's name is an important part of who that person is, and that the person and his or her name is to be treated with respect, make these name mobiles.

Have each child print his or her name in large block letters on a sheet of paper, making the letters wide enough to decorate the interiors with colorful designs. Cut out the letters. Use markers to decorate the letters, making squiggles, dots, stripes, plaid or other designs. Decorate both sides of the letters, then cover them with clear contact paper. Punch a hole in the top of each letter, and tie a piece of nylon thread through the hole, or slide a paper clip through the hole. Attach the name to a clothes hanger and hang it in the room.

New Kid on the Block

Divide the large group into two or more smaller groups. Give each group a role-play situation that involves a new kid moving onto the block, or starting in a classroom at school. Use actual situations if you are aware of them. Let the kids act out these situations, showing their feelings and responses. Then take time to talk about how the different people in the situations feel. Have you ever been in this situation? How did you feel? If you felt badly, what made you feel better?

Sailing on the Seven Cs

Focus: Understanding friendship

Social and Emotional Concepts:

➪ Friendship includes caring, consideration, commitment, communication, concern, curiosity, and cooperation.

➪ Actions sometimes speak louder than words.

➪ Friendship works best when we work and play at it.

A Book to Read and Talk About
Tacky is on the move, and his travels take him farther than he has ever been before. Find out where Tacky travels and who he meets in Nancy Lester's book, *Tacky in Trouble*.

Question and Answer Cards

In preparation for this activity prepare a set of index cards. On one side write one of the seven "C" words (caring, consideration, commitment, communication, concern, curiosity, and cooperation) on each card. On the other side, write the appropriate phrase that goes with the "C" word:

I show someone I care by . . .

When someone is a considerate person they . . .

Commitment means . . .

I like to communicate by . . .

One way to show concern to another person is to . . .

When I am curious, I . . .

One way that people cooperate is . . .

Begin by showing everyone the seven "C" words cards and reading them aloud together. Play the song. Talk about each "C" word, inviting kids to say what they think each of the words means based on what they heard in the song. Then use the phrase cards as sentence starters to encourage everyone to share their thoughts and ideas about what it means to be a friend.

Actions Speak Louder than Words

To explore how our actions show how we feel about ourselves and about others, involve the children in a simple game of charades. As they are able, have the children write on index cards the things they do in a typical day, one thing per card. For example, put the breakfast dishes in the dishwasher, play a game with friends, take out the trash, do homework, or walk to school with a friend. Collect the cards.

Talk about the saying "Actions speak louder than words." Then have a child, or partners, choose a card and pantomime what it says, using props from the room as needed. Have other kids guess the activity. Take time to talk about each example, emphasizing how the action can be a positive example.

Hands of Friendship

You will need tempera or finger paint, shallow pans or dishes, 9" x 12" construction paper, paint shirts, and crayons or markers.

Help the children make cheery cards for others who may be ill at home or in the hospital, or who may be sad because of a family tragedy. Demonstrate how to dip their hands into a shallow pan of paint and make two handprints on the top half of a horizontally folded piece of construction paper. When the paintings are dry, use crayons or markers to add stems and leaves below the hand prints to turn them into flowers. Add a get-well wish or other caring message to the cards and send them to someone who needs a friend.

Guess the Classmate

You will need three index cards per child and pencils.

This is a way to help students develop friendships by getting to know each other. Give three index cards to each person. Have the kids write one interesting fact about themselves on each card. Encourage the students to write something that others may not know about them. Collect the cards and mix them up.

When you need a short activity in the classroom, select one of the cards and read what's written on it. Have the students guess to which classmate that fact belongs. Another way to use the cards is to have students work together as a team to guess the classmate, scoring points for each correct guess.

The Gift of Giving

Focus: Giving the gift of love

Social and Emotional Concepts:

➪ Love grows when we give it to others.

➪ When someone shares with us, we want to share with them.

➪ The more love we give, the more we have to give away.

> **A Book to Read and Talk About**
> A classic book about giving is *The Giving Tree* by Shel Silverstein. What do the boy and the tree share throughout the years? Another book, *Reach Out and Give* by Cheri J. Meiners, shows us how to give to the world we live in.

Giving Smiles

For this activity you will need fast-drying clay or play dough, a rolling pin, straws, round and heart-shaped cookie cutters, coins, and twine, ribbon, or leather laces. To make play dough, mix together in a saucepan ½ cup salt, 1 cup flour, 1 Tablespoon cream of tartar, 1 Tablespoon oil, and 1 cup water. Cook over low heat, stirring continually until the mixture begins to form as dough. Add a few drops of food coloring if you like. Dump out the dough onto a paper-covered table and knead carefully to mix the color. Let cool. Store in an airtight container.

When we give happiness away, it grows and grows and grows! Make "smile tokens" to share happiness with others. Let the kids make as many tokens as they would like to give to others.

With a rolling pin, roll the clay or dough to a thickness of ½" to 1". The smile tokens can be cut into a number of free-form shapes or with the use of cookie cutters. Make a smile face on each token. You can also use coins or other objects pressed into the dough to make imprints (remove before the drying process). When a child is pleased with a design, use a straw to insert a hole at the top of the shape to add a ribbon or lace after the token dries. After the dough or clay has dried, tie twine, ribbon, or leather lace through the hole to make a hanging medallion.

Decorative Flowerpots

You will need clean dry terracotta flowerpots and saucers; acrylic paints; brushes; and fine-tipped, black, permanent markers.

Demonstrate how to paint different designs and shapes on the flowerpots with the acrylic paints. Have the kids make simple flower shapes, vines, leaves and even insects on the pots. When the paint is dry, outline the shapes and add details with the black pen. Use the black pen to add a favorite phrase from "The Gift of Giving." Plant a favorite plant, and give the decorative pot as a gift to a friend or family member. (This can be an excellent Mother's Day gift.)

Baking

You will need a favorite recipe that is easy to mix and make, the ingredients for the recipe, baking utensils, an oven, lunch-sized paper bags, clear plastic wrap or small plastic bags, hole punch, ribbon or yarn, and markers or crayons. If you can't, or don't want to, prepare the baked item from scratch, you could purchase prepared cookie dough for baking.

Let everyone help with mixing and baking your favorite cookie, brownie, or other recipe of goodies to share. (Be aware of students' food allergies, such as peanut butter or nuts.)

While the treats are baking, use the markers or crayons to decorate paper bags with drawings, friendship words, and creative designs. Fold down an inch of the paper bag tops and punch two holes so that ribbon or yarn can be threaded through the holes to tie the bags shut.

When the baked goods are out of the oven and cooled, put them in plastic bags or wrap them in plastic. Place two or three wrapped items in each paper bag and tie the bag with ribbon or yarn. Give the goodies away, but be sure to save a few for enjoying with your group.

To extend this activity, write about a time that you gave something to someone else. How did it make you feel to give a gift? Now think about a time that you got a gift from someone. Draw a picture of the gift you received and write a sentence about how you felt getting a gift.

Let 'Em Out

Focus: Handling feelings

Social and Emotional Concepts:

⇨ It is good to share our feelings with other people.

⇨ Sometimes it is hard to say how we really feel.

⇨ All kinds of feelings can be expressed to caring people.

A Book to Read and Talk About

Feelings by Aliki is a well-known book that can help young children identify the different feelings that all people have. Another fun book to read and talk about is *My Many Colored Days* by Dr. Seuss, where the colors of the days can sometimes reflect our feelings or mood.

My Feelings

You will need large sheets of paper, paints, brushes, and mirrors. An optional item is to have a poster, book, or other product that shows facial expressions of various feelings.

Feelings are real and feelings can change. How are you feeling right now? Talk about the different moods and feelings that the children have, and ask the children how they are feeling today. How many are feeling the same as someone else? Different? Encourage the children to make their faces show the different feelings they might experience. Use a feelings book or poster to further explore this topic. (One option is the "Feelings" poster available from Free Spirit Publishing.) Keep the poster available in the room to refer to often.

Set out the mirrors, paper, paints, and brushes. Allow everyone to experiment with facial expressions and then to paint a self-portrait of one feeling or mood. When finished, see if others can guess the feelings in the self-portraits. Hang the completed self-portraits in your "art gallery."

Lights! Camera! Action!

You will need a variety of silly hats or props, a digital camera (optional), and photo print paper (optional).

Let everyone try on the silly hats or props and talk about the moods and feelings they create. Some might be silly, like a clown hat, while others might be serious, like a graduation cap. Talk about how faces, arms, and whole bodies can show feelings. Let everyone choose a favorite item and wear it as they strike appropriate poses. If a digital camera is available, take pictures of everyone, print them, and make your own "feelings" poster to display.

Time for Popcorn

You will need to purchase or make popcorn in a variety of flavors, such as plain, butter, salted, caramel, cheese, and cinnamon sugar. You'll also need napkins and small paper plates.

Ask the children what flavors of popcorn they have tried. What is your favorite flavor? Do a taste test with the variety of popcorn flavors you have available. Serve one at a time on the plates and have kids guess what flavor it is. Encourage everyone to taste all the different flavors. What was the most popular flavor? Discuss that even though plain or butter and salted popcorn are good, sometimes it is fun to try a new flavor. In fact, that is kind of like all of the different moods and feelings that people have—if everyone was feeling the same way all the time, wouldn't life be boring? Expressing different feelings makes life interesting.

More and More Feelings

You will need Feelings in a Jar (available from Free Spirit Publishing), or a similar product.

Use the cards from *Feelings in a Jar* as a way to explore even more feelings than those the kids typically think of, such as courageous, witty, or suspicious. Let each person pull a feeling card from the jar and act it out for the rest of the group to guess what feeling it is. Talk about the feeling being portrayed and what might be appropriate ways for kids to express that feeling.

The Carousel Song

Focus: Understanding life's ups and downs

Social and Emotional Concepts:

➪ Things in life don't always go well.

➪ When something doesn't go right at first, you can try again.

➪ Mistakes are okay when you learn from them.

A Book to Read and Talk About
Life is full of ups and downs. Read about some of them in the Dr. Seuss book, *Oh, The Places You'll Go!*

What Places Will You Go?

You will need the book suggested above.

Talking about personal and group goals is a way to talk about life's ups and downs and, at the same time, strengthen a child's self-concept and build the group's cohesion.

Begin by reading *Oh, the Places You'll Go!* Follow the story with a discussion about what determines success. When do you think you are successful? When do things not go so well for you? What do you do if you fail? Help the children make a connection between setting goals and measuring success. Brainstorm goals for the group and record them for reference throughout the year.

To extend the activity, have the children set their own personal goals. This could be done in journals or in letters the kids write to themselves. The letters could be opened at a later time or end of the school year to see if the kids were successful at reaching their goals.

A Carousel Dance

You will need a CD player and CDs of different types of music.

Most kids love to move and dance. Play and listen to several different types of music, using *Ready to Rock Kids* and other CDs you may have available. Encourage everyone to really listen to the music and feel what kind of movements it is telling them to do. Listen to "The Carousel Song" and create a dance that imitates the motions in the song. Discuss what the children believe the song means, and use that understanding in the dance you create. Practice the dance, then perform it for your classmates, friends, or family.

Weaving Around

You will need small branches and assorted colors, sizes, and textures of strings, ribbons, and yarn.

Weaving is an activity that is fun to do, but it is often a challenge that requires kids to keep trying and to learn from their mistakes. Your kids may be familiar with paper weaving, but weaving with a branch and yarn can be a new experience.

Help kids tie one end of a piece of string or yarn to one twig that is part of a branch. Then criss-cross it back and forth to another twig on the branch in order to form the base on which they will weave. Be sure the ends of the string are tied securely to the branch. Encourage everyone to use a variety of textures and colors of yarns, strings, and ribbons to weave in and out on the branch base, tying the ends of each additional piece of material to the base. Help the children see that if they make a mistake, they can take out the yarn and try again. Display the completed weavings where everyone can enjoy them.

What Time Is It?

You will need index cards, markers or crayons, binder rings or key chain rings.

Talk about a typical day for your kids and the kind of schedule they have. One of life's greatest skills is learning to manage time, and we are never too young to learn how to do that. Choose a daily time frame, such as 8 A.M. to 8 P.M. Give everyone one card per hour with the particular time written at the top of the cards. Help the kids think about the things they typically do at those particular hours, and have them write or draw those things on the cards. Talk about how important routines and schedules are in our lives. When things do not always go as planned, what do we do?

When the 12 cards are completed, punch two holes in the top of each card for the binder rings or key chain rings and attach the cards together as an easy reminder or reference for learning a daily schedule.

The Golden Rule

Focus: Treat others as you would like to be treated

Social and Emotional Concepts:

⇨ The Golden Rule can help us make good decisions.

⇨ If you can't say something nice, don't say anything at all.

⇨ Teasing can hurt other's feelings.

A Book to Read and Talk About
The little bear is lonely on the shelf in the toy department. Will no one ever become his friend? One day a little girl visits the store, and Corduroy's life is changed forever. Read all about it in *Corduroy* by Don Freeman.

Golden Rule Bracelets

You will need elastic cord and assorted beads, some of them gold-colored. Cut a length of elastic that will comfortably fit around a child's wrist, being sure to leave enough cord to tie the ends together after the bracelet is finished.

Make bracelets to wear or share as reminders of treating other people as you would like to be treated. Begin by sorting the beads by shape and size. Once the beads are sorted, play "The Golden Rule" while the kids create their own designs or patterns for their bracelets by stringing beads on the elastic cord. When finished, tie the ends of the elastic together for them. As a reminder of how to treat others, each child can make one bracelet for himself or herself and another for a friend.

Thanks Stickers

You will need self-adhesive paper or large labels, fine-tip markers, ballpoint pens, and scissors to make "Thanks for being a friend" stickers.

To help reinforce the golden rule message on a daily basis, explain to the children that they will make "Thanks for being a friend" stickers that can be given to anyone they "catch" being a good friend to them. Plan to make a lot of stickers for use in the months ahead.

Cut interesting shapes from the self-adhesive paper. On the shapes write "Thanks for being a friend," and then color and decorate the sticker as desired. At designated times during the day, ask the kids who deserves one of their stickers. Let children give stickers to others and tell how they showed friendship.

Spoon Puppet Actors

You will need plastic spoons; scraps of felt or fabric; yarn; permanent, fine-tip markers; glue; and scissors.

Set out the puppet making materials and invite the kids to create puppets to represent themselves and their friends, using plastic spoons as the puppet body. The bowl of the spoon is the face. Use the markers to make facial features. Add yarn hair and use fabric to "dress" the puppet. As the children are working, talk about how we treat other people and how other people treat us. Let the kids use the completed puppets to act out situations when someone treated them as they would like to be treated, or when they wish someone had treated them differently. Acting out and talking about these events can help kids know how to react in real life situations.

Learning Good Manners

You will need a large puppet or stuffed animal.

Good manners are important in how we treat others. Use a puppet or stuffed animal, such as a bear, as the vehicle for talking about manners. Talk about examples of good manners and what we do, and don't do, when we are polite to each other. Have the children take turns thinking of one good manner and then teaching it to the puppet or stuffed animal. Talk about the manners and how the children can demonstrate good manners with friends and family.

Same and Different Too

Focus: Celebrating diversity

Social and Emotional Concepts:

⇨ We are all the same in some ways, but in other ways different.

⇨ It's fun to share what we have in common.

⇨ Our differences are interesting too.

> **A Book to Read and Talk About**
> *Sitting Ducks* by Michael Bedard is a book that showcases the diversity in a friendship, and how important it proves to be. *Accept and Value Each Person* by Cheri J. Meiners is a book that helps introduce children to the diverse world and culture we live in.

Fingerprint/Handprint Poster

You will need pencils, paper scraps, clear tape, drawing paper, tempera or finger paints, and paintbrushes.

There is no more unique feature to each person in the world than his or her fingerprint or handprint. To make handprint posters, paint a child's hand, then help him or her spread the fingers apart wide and press down on the paper to make the print.

Add fingerprints to the handprint by having the kids scribble with the pencil on paper scraps, creating a heavy section of pencil marks. Then rub a finger over the pencil marks to transfer the pencil lead to the finger. Press a piece of clear tape on the dirty finger. Peel the tape off and press it on the paper; now you should be able to see the fingerprint. Have the kids try making all of their fingerprints to compare the variety of shapes and sizes. While we are all alike in many ways, we have uniquely different hand and finger prints.

Sock Sort

You will need a large number of assorted pairs of socks—many different styles, sizes, colors, etc.

This is a good activity to use to start a conversation about likenesses and differences. Set the pile of socks in the center of the group. Talk about what the words *same* and *different* mean. Let everyone work together to sort the socks. At first, it may seem easy to sort, but encourage different ways to sort after the initial try. For example, you can sort by finding pairs, but you can also sort by color, size, texture, stripes, and so on.

A good book to read as part of this activity is called *A Pair of Socks* by Lois Ehlert, where different ways to sort and classify are clearly pointed out.

Same and Different Tapestry

You will need pencils, construction paper, scissors, glue, different colors of yarn, markers, glitter glue (optional), and a large sheet of poster board.

Have everyone trace their hands or feet on construction paper, and then cut them out. Line the edge with glue and lay yarn over the glue. On the hand or foot write the child's name with a marker or with glitter glue. Attach all the hands to a sheet of poster board for a group tapestry. Title the tapestry "Same and Different."

Family Picture Puzzles

You will need each child to supply a family picture, rubber cement or glue, clear adhesive paper, scissors, and poster board.

Even in a family it is easy to see things that are the same and different about family members. Make a list of those things using your own family as an example. Then invite the children to do the same with their families.

With younger children you may want to focus especially on physical attributes, and with older children you may want to move into the likes and dislikes of family members. Conclude with the fact that each family is really a combination of many elements, including things that are the same and things that are different.

Making a family puzzle will reinforce the idea that each of our families has many different parts to it, and all the parts combine to make one family. Carefully glue the family picture to poster board. When the glue is dry, cover the entire picture with clear adhesive paper. Leaving a small border, cut around the edge of the picture. Turn over the picture and draw puzzle piece shapes on the poster board in a size that the children can successfully handle. Cut out the pieces to make your very own family puzzle.

Celebrate Differences

You will need the book The Sneeches, *or a video of the story.*

After hearing or watching the story, ask the children to name all the things that were different about the two groups of Sneeches. Talk about how the groups treated each other. Do you think it was fair the way the Sneeches without stars were treated? What did they do to look like the Star Bellied Sneeches. What happened when everyone was looking alike? Do you think people ever act like Sneeches?

In pairs, have the kids name five things, or more, about themselves that are different from each other. Talk about how differences make us unique individuals, and how, even though we may have some differences, every one of us is important.

What You Can Do

Focus: Learning new things
Social and Emotional Concepts:

⇨ New things can sometimes be scary.

⇨ Trying is the first step in learning something new.

⇨ Learning is fun when things are broken down into small steps.

A Book to Read and Talk About
Tomie dePaola is one of the best-loved artists and children's book authors of our time. His simple drawings enhance the stories that children love to hear again and again. *The Art Lesson* tells the story of how he wanted to be an artist from the time he was a little boy, and how he grew up and learned along the way.

Mystery Box Guessing

You will need a large cardboard box, scissors or knife, and items of various textures to place inside the box.

In one end of the box, cut a hole that is just large enough for a hand to slip inside. Place one item at a time into the box and let the kids take turns slipping a hand inside to feel what the item is. Encourage the kids to not be afraid of the unknown, but to give this a try. Don't let anyone tell what their guess is until everyone has had a chance to take a turn.

Hula Hoops and Jump Ropes

You will need hula hoops, jump ropes, and other simple play equipment, and bubble gum.

Give everyone the opportunity to try and learn a new skill. Have the kids who already know how to use a hula hoop, jump rope, or blow bubble gum bubbles demonstrate these

Sharing Friends

Focus: Including others

Social and Emotional Concepts:

⇨ Sometimes it's fun to play alone, and sometimes it's better with others.

⇨ Lots of activities are more fun with more people.

⇨ Sharing friends can make everyone happy.

> **A Book to Read and Talk About**
> Are there any better friends in the world than Frog and Toad? There are many books about their adventures together, but *Frog and Toad Are Friends* by Arnold Lobel is a great book to share with a friend of your own. Other good books about friendship include *Who Will Be My Friend?* by Syd Hoff, and *Do You Want to Be My Friend?* by Eric Carle.

skills to everyone else, or demonstrate these skills yourself. Have fun trying new things and laughing and learning together.

Learning Buddies

It is often frightening for children to make new friends. Find another teacher at school who will work with you. Pair together students from each classroom who do not know each other and arrange for weekly meetings. The first time the students are together, have them interview each other with questions you help them prepare in advance. The second time the classes meet together, plan activities that allow for interaction, such as games, art projects, or working together on homework. As the meetings continue, encourage the kids to write and illustrate a story about their new friends.

Often successful in schools is the concept of pairing together older students with younger students. This can function as a kind of big sister/big brother program where older students can be mentors for younger kids and help them learn about their new school. With administrative support, and teacher enthusiasm, this can become a successful school-wide activity.

Friendship Books

You will need one or more of the books named above, markers, and chart paper.

After reading a book about friendship, have the children name the main characters as you list them on chart paper. With help from the kids, under the character's name, list the traits that suggest he or she might be a good friend. If any character has negative traits, you could list those in a different color. Then have the kids think of a personal friend or classmate who has one or more of the positive traits. Give the children an opportunity to compliment the friends they named.

Fun in Numbers

Some things are just more fun, and easier, when done with others. Try some simple games that take two people, such as a wheelbarrow race, a three-legged race, or simple chores. This is one way of showing kids how some things are easier to do with two people than alone.

Add to the fun by having two children see how long they can bounce a beach ball up in the air together. Then let them experience the added benefit of a third child, then a fourth child, and so on.

Friendship Pennant

You will need poster board, pencils, crayons or markers, and scissors.

Make a friendship pennant to display in your room. Cut a large pennant shape from poster board. Sketch out your friendship pennant design to reflect things about a specific friend and the things you like to do together. You might want to include your name, your friend's name, pictures or drawings of some of your favorite things, or any other features you want to add that makes this pennant about friendship. When you are happy with your design, color the final product. As an alternate method, you may want to make the pennant with fabric (such as felt) and fabric paints.

Hang your friendship pennant on a wall or door in your room to remind you of how good it feels to have a friend.

Friendly Food

You will need English muffins, pizza sauce, pizza toppings of your choice, an oven, baking pans, hot pads, spatula, paper plates, and napkins.

Have students cooperate to prepare a friendly, delicious snack or lunch. Assign jobs to pairs of students for the preparation of the mini pizzas, setting the table, serving the food, and cleaning up afterwards. Talk about working together to get a positive result.

Preheat an oven to 350 degrees. Split the English muffins into two halves, then spread pizza sauce on top. Add cheese and your favorite pizza toppings. Put the mini pizzas on baking trays and bake for about 10 minutes. When finished, let the pizzas cool slightly before sharing with a friend.

Cooperative Learning

Students can demonstrate friendship and cooperation with a small group activity requiring teamwork. Give groups of three to five students the assignment to explore the topic of friendship and prepare a report for the class. The groups will each need to decide a job, or jobs, for each person in the group. For example, the jobs may include research on great friends in history, drawing a poster that encourages friendship or a series of posters that speak to the qualities of friendship, preparing a final report, creating a photo display or video of friends, and whatever the group decides is important. The group should also decide how to report to the class and who will do that. Help each group to figure out how they can make decisions and solve problems that may arise as they work together.

I Don't Understand

Focus: Asking questions

Social and Emotional Concepts:

⇨ There are no questions that are wrong to ask.

⇨ When we ask questions, we learn new things.

⇨ Sometimes a child's question expresses a wish.

A Book to Read and Talk About
Amazing Grace by Mary Hoffman is a book about Grace, her dreams, her friendships, and the adults who encourage her.

Flights of Fantasy

Have the children close their eyes and imagine a special place that they would like to fly to. Then have them describe this place through writing or talking about it, and then draw a picture of it.

Magic Wishing Well

Using small index cards, have the children draw a picture of themselves that shows some magical ability that they would wish for. Place the cards in a box (the wishing well) and shake the box. One-by-one pull the cards out of the wishing well and let each child share his or her wish.

Simple Science

You will need the assorted items suggested with each experiment for the ones you choose to do.

Science is one of the coolest things! Let the children try these simple experiments to see if they can answer the questions and understand what happens each time.

★ Blow air through a straw onto your hand. Can you feel the air? Can you hear it? Can you see it?

★ Put a penny on a saucer. Use an eyedropper to add drops of water to the penny. How many drops can you add before it spills over?

★ Put a piece of waxed paper on a table. Sprinkle water drops on the paper. What happens? Why do you think it does this?

★ Experiment with a magnet. What can the magnet pick up? What doesn't it pick up? Do you know why?

★ Put a dot of nail polish on your fingernail. Wait a few days. What happens? Does the mark move? Why?

★ Put water in a glass. Drop in some red food coloring. What happens? Why?

Thank-You Bookmark

You will need drawing paper, markers, clear adhesive paper, glitter, sequins and other "sparkly" confetti, hole punch, ribbon, scissors, and bowls.

Make a bookmark for a teacher to say "thanks" for answering your questions and helping you learn. Put the sparkly items in bowls and set them on a table. Cut drawing paper into 2" x 7" strips. Have the child write a thank you message to his or her teacher on the strip. Add the sparkly items to decorate the bookmark. When finished with the design, help the child cover both sides of the bookmark with clear adhesive paper. Punch a hole in the top and tie a ribbon to finish the bookmark. Share your gift with a favorite teacher.

What If?

Use this activity to get kids thinking and using their imaginations. When you have a few minutes to spare, or during transition times, pose one of these questions:

- ★ What if you got to teach this class and make all the rules?
- ★ What if television had never been invented?
- ★ What if we could travel in outer space?
- ★ What if we had to use ice cubes for money?
- ★ What if it really did rain cats and dogs?
- ★ What if you had four arms?
- ★ What if you were born old and then got younger every year?
- ★ What if you never went to school?

Have students create their own "what if" questions for others to use. They might have fun asking questions that help discover how specific things work. Also encourage the students to ask the questions they might otherwise be afraid or embarrassed to ask. You can have them ask for help from adults or older students to find answers for their questions, or you may want them to find some answers by themselves.

What if the world were flat?

What if people were all the same?

What if we didn't have toes?

Cleanup Time

Focus: Taking responsibility for your things

Social and Emotional Concepts:

⇨ We should all take care of our things.

⇨ It's more fun when people work together.

⇨ Cleaning up includes returning things to where they belong.

A Book to Read and Talk About
It is important to care for the things we have. In *Arthur Clean Your Room*, Arthur learns about the importance of taking care of his own things. In *Arthur's Pet Business*, Arthur sets out to prove to his parents that he is responsible enough to have a pet of his own.

Cleanup Games

You will need a messy room, toy baskets or boxes, and a timer.

It isn't hard to make cleanup fun. Try one of these cleanup games to encourage everyone's participation.

- ★ Playing the song "Cleanup Time," use the pause button on your CD player to pause the song at different times. Have the children "freeze" right where they are whenever the music stops and continue cleaning when it starts again.
- ★ Beat the clock: Set the timer, or use an egg timer, to see how fast you can pick up a mess.
- ★ Color pick up: Let each person choose a favorite color and pick up all the items with that color.

★ Categories: Let students choose the categories of things to pick up. For example, first pick up everything that has wheels, then everything that is rectangular, and so on. This reinforces learning and cooperation, as well as gets the room cleaned up.

Toy Box Treasures

You will need storage boxes, baskets, or tubs; and a digital camera, photo paper, and printer (or adhesive labels and markers).

To help organize toys and to always have a place for playthings, collect similar size containers. Help kids categorize the different types of toys they have. Take a photo of each category (such as blocks, dolls, cars, etc.) with a digital camera. Print the photos and fasten each one to the front of a container. (If not using a camera, have the kids draw the items on labels to attach to the containers.) When it is time to clean up, toys pictured on the container go in that container.

Recycling Fun

You will need boxes, bags, or other containers for recycled items.

Involve kids and everyone in recycling at home and school. If you don't have recycling containers already, make and decorate your own. Find out what kinds of items your community recycles. Label your containers appropriately, such as glass, paper, aluminum, and plastic. Learn how recycled items are used again. Work together to recycle and see how much you can eliminate in your weekly garbage pick up.

Soldier of Peace

Focus: Being a peacemaker
Social and Emotional Concepts:
⇨ Peace begins with you.
⇨ Everyone can make the world a better place.
⇨ Showing love to others is the way to peace.

A Book to Read and Talk About
The opposite of peace is violence, and with a world that seems to have no end to the violent images we see every day, it is refreshing to read this simple, classic book about Ferdinand the bull, who just loved to sit and admire the beautiful flowers. You can read about Ferdinand in the book by Munro Leaf, *The Story of Ferdinand*.

Star Mobiles

You will need foil or Mylar paper and a star-shaped cookie cutter; or white glue, glitter, and wax paper; scissors; fishing line or nylon thread; hole punch; and a plastic clothes hanger or wooden dowel.

Make star mobiles to remind kids that they can be shining examples of peace and love in the world. One method is to trace around star-shaped cookie cutters on foil or Mylar paper. If possible, make several different sizes, and then cut out the stars. Punch a hole in the top of each star and tie it to a clothes hanger or dowel.

Another fun way to make stars is to draw a thick star shape with white glue on wax paper. Before the glue dries, cover it entirely with glitter. Let this dry thoroughly over night. Carefully peel the glitter star from the wax paper. Tie a length of thread through the star and hang it from the ceiling or hang several stars on the hanger or dowel.

Peace Sign Medallion

You will need pipe cleaners and ribbon or yarn.

Use pipe cleaners to make the universal peace sign shape. Tie a length of yarn or ribbon through it to make a medallion that you can wear.

Love Sun-Catchers

You will need waxed paper, several colors of tissue paper, pre-cut letters, scissors, newspapers, an iron, hole punch, and string or yarn.

Use pre-cut letters to spell out the phrase "love one another" in the center of a piece of waxed paper. Around the words arrange torn pieces of tissue paper, which should overlap each other and could partially overlap the words. Cover this entire arrangement with another piece of waxed paper. Carefully place this entire arrangement between layers of newspapers. Iron the newspapers until the waxed paper seals together. Trim the waxed paper into a square or circle and hang it in a window to let the sun shine through and proclaim the message of love and peace.

Peace Marchers

You will need a CD player, the Ready to Rock Kids *CD, and rhythm instruments (optional).*

Have the children talk about the ways they would like to see more peace in their community and the world. Then ask them about the small steps they might take to help. Play "Soldier of Peace" and other songs, and let the kids march and dance around the room for peace. Add rhythm instruments for the kids to play along with the music.

To extend the activity, help the kids brainstorm ways to make a difference in their own school, community, or even beyond. Choose one way to involve the kids in making a difference. This could turn into an ongoing project, or one that involves others in the school or local community. It may be a food drive or a bake sale; choose a project that helps kids see the amount of effort that has to be put into it to achieve tangible and intangible results. At the end of the project, talk about the different ways they were able to "see" the results. Part of the learning is to see that making the world a better place requires persistence. The children should feel good about the immediate results of the project, such as being able to collect a lot of food or money to reach their goals. Then they also need to realize that they must continue to work at it to get the desired results for the ones who benefit from their help.

The Ready to Rock Stars

Front Row: Addison, Briggs, Olivia, Alexandra, Sam. **Back Row:** Nya, Emma, Anya, Allison

Dr. Mac **Lois** **Eje** **Brian** **Craig**

For more information about Ready to Rock Kids, write to Free Spirit Publishing, 217 Fifth Avenue North, Suite 200, Minneapolis, MN 55409, or visit www.freespirit.com. You can reach Dr. Mac at www.MacSongs.com or by writing to him at Dr. Mac Productions, P.O. Box 5772, Santa Barbara, CA 93150.

Also available separately:

Ready to Rock Kids Volume 2 Music CD
by Dr. Mac & Friends
Twelve songs, lyrics sheet, $14.95

Ready to Rock Kids Volume 1
(Activity Book and Music CD)
by Dr. Mac & Friends
Build social and emotional skills (and brainpower) with upbeat, inviting songs by a child psychologist and award-winning songwriter. Musically sophisticated, professionally produced songs teach and reinforce caring, sharing, responsibility, friendship, expressing feelings, positive thinking, valuing diversity, honesty, and more. The kid-friendly lyrics and beats you can dance to make learning fun. Adults like these tunes as much as kids do. (Teachers and parents, they won't drive you crazy.) The companion book includes activities that reinforce key concepts, reproducible activity pages, and complete lyrics.
48 pp., illustrated, 24 reproducible handouts. PreK–grade 3.

Ready to Rock Kids Volume 1 Music CD
by Dr. Mac & Friends
1. Welcome to the Big Parade
2. Give It Back
3. Let Me Play Too
4. The Magic Word
5. Everybody Wants to Find a Friend
6. Go Away Bad Thoughts
7. Talkin' About Talkin'
8. Diplodocus
9. Practice
10. Don't Say Maybe
11. Happy as Happy Can Be
12. Together

Twelve songs, lyrics sheet, $14.95

Visit freespirit.com to hear samples from *Ready to Rock Kids Volume 1*.

Other Great Materials from Free Spirit

Just Because I Am
A Child's Book of Affirmation
by Lauren Murphy Payne, M.S.W., illustrated by Claudia Rohling, M.S.W.
Warm, simple words and enchanting full-color illustrations strengthen and support children's self-esteem. Ideal for early elementary, preschool, childcare, and the home. For ages 3–8.
$8.95; 32 pp.; softcover; color illust.; 7⅝" x 9¼"

The Best Behavior Series
Simple words and delightful full-color illustrations guide children to choose peaceful, positive behavior. Selected titles are available in two versions: a durable board book for ages baby to preschool, and a longer, more in-depth paperback for ages 4 to 7. Kids, parents, and teachers love these award-winning books. Each includes a special section of tips and ideas for parents and caregivers.
Paperbacks: $11.95; 40 pp.; color illust.; 9" x 9"; ages 4–7.
Board Books: $7.95; 24 pp.; color illust.; 7" x 7"; ages baby–preschool.

Other titles include:

Tails Are Not for Pulling	Words Are Not for Hurting
Tails Are Not for Pulling Board Book	Words Are Not for Hurting Board Book
Germs Are Not for Sharing	Teeth Are Not for Biting Board Book
Germs Are Not for Sharing Board Book	Feet Are Not for Kicking Board Book

We Can Get Along
A Child's Book of Choices
by Lauren Murphy Payne, M.S.W., illustrated by Claudia Rohling, M.S.W.
Children need help learning how to get along with others at school, in the neighborhood, and on the playground. They need to know that they have the power to make good choices. In simple, affirming words and exuberant full-color illustrations, We Can Get Along teaches essential conflict resolution and peacemaking skills—think before you speak or act, treat others the way you want to be treated—in a way that young children can understand. For ages 3–8.
$9.95; 36 pp.; softcover; illust; 7⅝" x 9¼"

The Learning to Get Along® Series
Social and emotional competence is key to success in school and in life. Young children need to learn how to deal with their emotions, make positive choices, solve problems, resolve conflicts, resist impulsive behavior, form relationships, work cooperatively, and more. Our Learning to Get Along series helps parents, teachers, childcare providers, and anyone else who cares about kids teach basic social and emotional skills. Written for ages 4 to 8, meant to be read aloud, each book focuses on a specific skill. Each includes a special section for adults. All are positive, practical, realistic, and sound—just what you'd expect from a Free Spirit series.
each $10.95; 40 pp.; softcover; color illust.; 9" x 9"

Safe & Caring Schools PreK–2
by Katia Petersen, Ph.D.
Research shows that the formula for success in today's schools is SEAL: Social, Emotional, and Academic Learning. Safe & Caring Schools (SCS) materials incorporate social/emotional learning into daily academic instruction, improving classroom dynamics, reducing behavior problems, and building strong character and academic success. All SCS materials have been extensively classroom-tested. Activities comply with standards while promoting selfawareness, social skills, and responsible decision-making.
$29.95; softcover; illust; 8½" x 11"

Other titles include:

Be Careful and Stay Safe	Respect and Take Care of Things
Be Polite and Kind	Share and Take Turns
Join In and Play	Talk and Work It Out
Know and Follow Rules	Try and Stick with It
Listen and Learn	Understand and Care
Reach Out and Give	When I Feel Afraid

To place an order or to request a free catalog of SELF-HELP FOR KIDS® and SELF-HELP FOR TEENS® materials, please write, call, email, or visit our Web site:

Free Spirit Publishing Inc.
217 Fifth Avenue North • Suite 200 • Minneapolis, MN 55401-1299
toll-free 800.735.7323 • local 612.338.2068 • fax 612.337.5050
help4kids@freespirit.com • www.freespirit.com